Adam Raccoon
and the
Flying Machine

Rachel

Glen Keane

Chariot Books™
David C. Cook Publishing Co.

To Linda

Chariot Books™ is an imprint of David C. Cook
Publishing Co.
David C. Cook Publishing Co., Elgin, Illinois 60120
David C. Cook Publishing Co., Weston, Ontario

ADAM RACCOON AND THE FLYING MACHINE
© 1989 by Glen Keane for text and illustrations

First printing, 1989

93 92   5 4

Library of Congress Cataloging-in-Publication Data

Keane, Glen, 1954-
   Adam Raccoon and the flying machine / Glen Keane.
      p.   cm.
   Summary: When he tries to build an airplane without
reading the instructions, Adam Raccoon soon learns that
"doing what feels right" is not always the correct way to
proceed.
   ISBN 1-55513-287-1
   [1. Raccoons—Fiction.   2. Conduct of life—Fiction.]
I. Title.
PZ7.K2173Acf   1989   [E]—dc19   88-17006
                                          CIP
                                          AC

High above the oak trees,
Sam, the little sparrow,
twirled and looped
through the air,

. . . Landing on a glider that Adam Raccoon had just finished building. "Ready to try it out?" Sam asked cheerfully.

"Yep, now I'll be able to fly like you, Sam."

Puffing and panting, Adam and
Sam pushed and pulled the glider
to the top of a very high cliff.

"All set!" Adam said, as Sam gave
him a final nudge.

As quickly as the glider
flew, it dropped,
leaving Adam
floating in midair.

He fell into the arms of King Aren, who was passing by at that very moment. "You'll never fly that way, Adam. But I may have just the thing you need."

And King Aren
led Adam and Sam
up a high mountain
to his storehouse
of wonderful treasures.

As King Aren opened the massive door, a bright light shone from within.

Adam and Sam stood amazed at the many strange and wonderful things they saw.

Soon King Aren
returned pushing a
large crate.

"What's that?"
Adam shouted
excitedly.

"You'll see as soon
as you put it together."

"All right! No problem!" Adam said as he scrambled onto the crate.

"Hold on, Adam. You'll need this instruction book to show you how to do it."

"You'll also need
someone to help
explain it to you.
Meet Ernest.
Be sure to listen to him."

After King Aren left, they went to
the business of opening the crate.
They tugged and pulled with all of
their might, and suddenly . . .

The crate burst open, sending the
three flying.

Ernest handed Adam the instruction book. "I think we'd better start here."

Adam started to read. " 'Find Section A and screw in Bolt 32 to Air Turbine D.' Ah, this is gonna take too long," Adam sighed.

"Of course it will!" said the professor, who strolled out from behind the bushes. "What do you expect when you do something the old-fashioned way?"

"We have the New Way now," he said, tossing the book into the bushes. "There's one simple rule. Do whatever feels right to you."

Much to Ernest's dismay, Adam started sticking whatever part onto whichever piece felt right to him.

Soon King Aren stopped by to see how things were going. "Where's the book, Adam?"

"Oh, that book was old fashioned. The professor showed me the New Way."

"I can't watch," King Aren said, as
Adam continued to build.

"King Aren, I'm done!" Adam shouted. "Isn't it great?"

"Well, Adam, what is it?" King Aren asked as he investigated the odd-looking contraption.

"It's a Flying Machine, of course," Adam replied.

"Oh, but the professor said it's safe. Right, professor?"

"That's right. Safer than standing on the ground," he answered hiding behind a tree.

"Want to ride with me?" Adam asked.

"I'd love to, but I . . . er . . . uh . . .
just remembered I've got some
important reading to do. Good luck!"

"I'll go, I'll go!" Sam volunteered.
He hopped in back as Adam started
the countdown. "10 . . . 9 . . . 8 . . ."

With a roar the machine took off,
wildly out of control, cutting a path
through Master's Wood.

"Help!" Adam screamed as animals dove for cover.

The machine
climbed high
into the sky
like a rocket,
far above
the clouds.

Adam frantically
tried to gain control,
pulling switches and
hitting buttons.

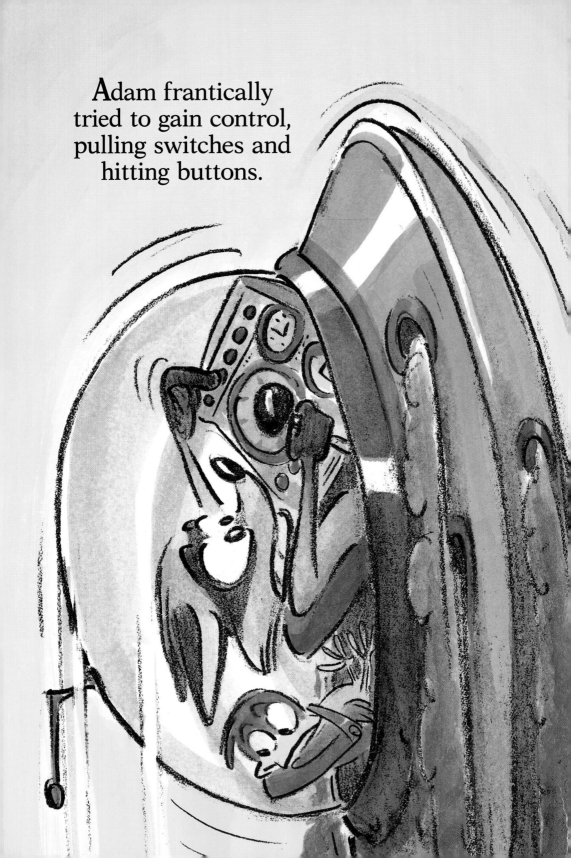

Suddenly
the ship turned
and plummeted
toward earth.

SPLASH! As the water settled, everyone watched for Adam and Sam to surface.

"Look out below!" Up above they saw Sam flapping his wings with all his might, clinging to Adam who was in a faint.

Dropping into King Aren's arms
the groggy raccoon awoke.
"Mayday! Mayday! We're going down!"

"Adam, you're back on the ground,"
the king said gently.

Hopping out of the king's arms, Adam ran to Ernest's side. "Oh, please give me another chance, King Aren. I'll follow the book and listen to Ernest this time, I promise."

King Aren agreed.
The next day the
flying machine
was pulled out of
the lake.

They started to
build once again.

Adam was surprised
at how much
he enjoyed
the hard work.

Weeks later as King Aren was taking his daily walk he was startled by a voice. "Hello down there. This is the X-25 Jet Hawk calling King Aren."

High above the trees Adam was hovering in his new Flying Machine. "Adam, you did it!" King Aren shouted.

"Not by myself," he replied, holding up the book with Sam and Ernest sitting beside him. "Now let's see what it can do!"

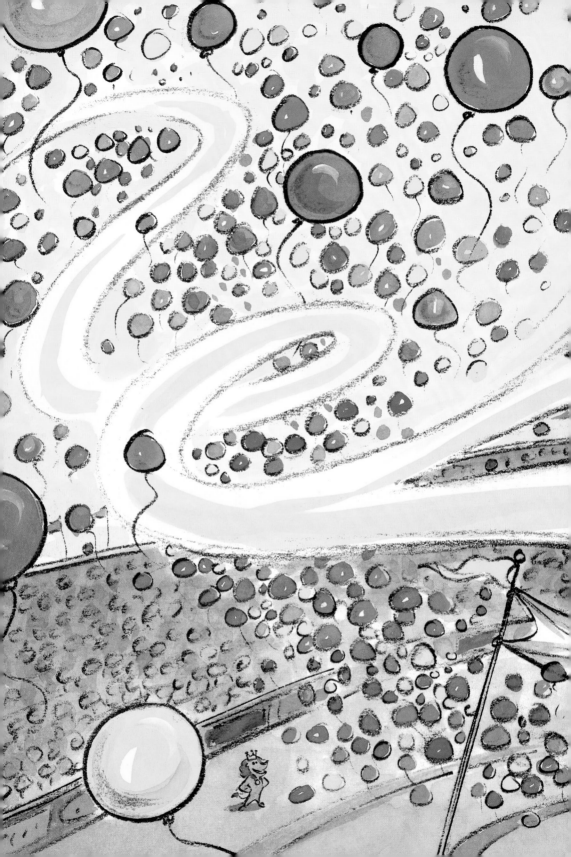

Then Adam, Sam, and Ernest gave the greatest air show that anyone in Master's Wood had ever seen.

REMEMBER THE STORY

Your word is a lamp to my feet and a light for my path.
Psalm 119:105 (NIV)

- What did King Aren plan for Adam to build?
- What happened the first time Adam tried to build the flying machine?
- Why didn't Adam use the instruction book?
- If you were Adam, what would you have said to the professor?
- What instruction book has God given us?
- God's Word doesn't teach us to build a flying machine. What does it teach us?
- What happens when we don't follow God's Word?
- What happens when we do follow God's Word?
- If you were Adam, what would you tell your friends you learned from this adventure?